MEET SANDY GULL

WRITTEN BY

MARY J. STALLER

ILLUSTRATED BY JIM HUNT

For my family, you are my heart and my happiness. Thank you for loving me always and for supporting me unconditionally.

For my friends and coworkers, your smiles and kindness will live in my heart always.

For my illustrator, thank you for making my characters come to life just the way I'd imagined!

 www.trafford.com

North America & international
toll-free: 1 888 232 4444 (USA & Canada)
phone: 250 383 6864 • fax: 812 355 4082

Mickey stood on the warm soft beach and wiggled his toes in the sand.
A boogie board under one arm and a chocolate pretzel in his hand,
He munched and he crunched on that sweet made by his gram.
A big bold seagull stood nearby; wanting that pretzel he stared with a sigh.

Mickey skipped over so he could stand
next to that bird but he kicked up the sand.

"Hey!" squawked the bird, for the sand stung his face."
Watch it my friend; this is not a race!"

"I'm sorry," said Mickey and he lowered his head.
"I'm okay," the bird said, then ran his beak through his feathe
"As long as we eat that last chocolate pretzel together!"

Mickey grinned. "Sure! There's plenty for two.
Come over here and I'll share it with you."

"Hello my friend and how do you do?
My name is Sandy Gull and I'm glad to meet you."

"Come with me and we'll have some fun.
I'll tell you some stories as we stroll in the sun."

"Look out for pesky footprints in the sand.
Some are quite small but some are quite grand!"

"I'm a bit of a rascal that's part of my charm.
Don't be afraid. I don't mean any harm."
"I'm a likeable bird, I must admit."
Mickey nodded his head then decided to sit.

"It's a glorious day. Get up now let's play!"
"Go grab your board and we'll take to the ocean.
We'll ride the crests of the waves, so rub on some lotion!"

"Alright!" exclaimed Mickey and he reached for his board.
He raised his face to the clouds and watched his friend soar.

"Here I am! I'm way up in the sky.
I can see for miles. I can fly high!"

Sandy Gull circled above Mickey's head.
Mickey straddled his board and waved to his friend.

The bird caught sight of the smallest sea creature.
A little red crab, he decided to tease her.
He dove straight down and with a splash,
Sandy came up with that crab in a flash!

Mickey watched as he flew toward the land
and carefully laid his catch on the sand.

Feeling quite pleased Sandy gave his feathers a nip.
He wandered the beach with a walk, walk, walk dip.
Mickey followed behind with a walk, walk, jump skip.

"Look over there!" Sandy Gull pointed his wing.
"Hurry up fast for I can't lose sight of that thing!"

The gull was so excited he began to shake.
"That luster, such gleam! It cannot be a mistake!"

Mickey looked around so he could see
just what made that seagull fill with such glee.
Children played with sand buckets and toys.
Babies giggled and laughed with pure joy.
Daddies played with wiffle balls and bats.
Mommies sunned in pretty straw hats.

"Right over there, that pretty young lady,
under the umbrella all nice
and shady."

"See there the brand
new orange beach bag?
The one that still has the
dangling price tag."

Zzzz

"My heart is beating oh so fast!
A shiny bag of potato chips at long last!"

"Potato chips, chocolate pretzels and sweet ice cream cones
are Sandy Gull's very FAVORITES," he moaned.

"Gulls love all those tasty things. Who knew?
My gram makes chocolate pretzels every day around two!"

Proudly Mickey bragged and stuck out his chest.
"That's delightful!" admired the gull. "We shall remain friends
very best!"

SQUAAAWK! EH! EH! Eh! Eh!

Mickey grinned at the sound he'd just heard.
"You sound like you're laughing, but that is absurd!
I never heard laughter come out of a bird."

"I'll tell you a secret if you come close to me."
Mickey liked secrets so he bent down on one knee.

He cupped his hand around his ear.
Just to be sure nobody else would hear.

"Seagulls practice that noise while we stand on the beaches.
But sometimes our laughter just sounds like loud screeches!"

"Did you think that I forgot why we're standing in this spot?
I never would and I did not!"
His attention was back to the potato chips in a shot!

11

Sandy hobbled toward the orange beach tote.
He stepped right up close and then cleared his throat.
He watched her a moment and when she didn't move,
he figured he'd better get on his groove.

That seagull began to bob and to weave.
He danced back and forth, Mickey could not believe!
Sandy grunted and scratched at his head.
He turned and looked at his young friend.

"I am confused! This cannot be right!
Why is this lady not being polite?"

The corners of Mickey's mouth turned down.
He shrugged his shoulders and watched with a frown.

Turning back to the lady, the gull stood quite straight.
He tilted his head in his most sincere trait.

"Mickey the sand is so nice and warm.
It does me no good to dance and perform."

"The lady has fallen sound asleep!
It's the only explanation. She's fallen quite deep."

"Of course she could not resist my charm.
But the sand is just so soothing and warm."

Mickey moved closer and took a good look.
"I think she fell asleep while reading her book."

"Wait my friend, would you be so kind
as to wake her up and if you wouldn't mind. . .
Request a potato chip for me?
No WAIT! You'd better ask her for three
or four, or maybe some more!"

Mickey looked at the lady and his cheeks went flush.
He turned his head and continued to blush.

"My you are shy," the seagull said.
Mickey kicked sand and nodded his head.

"Do not fret my little friend.
For this is nowhere near the end!"

"I, Sandy Gull, will take care of this.
It'll all be over in a zip!"

And off he went with a walk, walk, walk dip!

Sandy gave the bag a poke.
And for a moment he thought the lady woke!

He made a SNATCH for that shiny foil bag
and caught his beak on that white price tag!

"Help me my friend for I've hit quite a snag!"

Mickey looked at him and smirked.

Stealing should never EVER work!

Just then the lady sat upright
and saw the seagull's nasty plight.

"Now just what were you trying to do
when you got yourself in such a stew?"

Sandy was sure she already knew.

"I'm really sorry," the bird said with a sigh.
Mickey could see a tear fill his eye.

"I cannot be friends with someone who steals.
If you are hungry Gram will make you a meal.

"Sandy Gull stood oh so still
while the lady so gently freed up his bill.

He rubbed his feathers against his beak,
grateful again to be able to speak.

"Please don't say this is the end.
Tell me I can make amends
and we can all be the best of friends."

Sandy Gull tilted his head and looked sad.
For only a moment and then he looked glad.

For Mickey could never stay very mad
at a funny old bird who wasn't so bad.

Sandy held out his wing for Mickey to shake.
The boy slipped and pulled out one feather by mistake.

"OUCH!" Squawked the bird, his beak toward the sky.
"Be careful, I need those feathers to fly!"

"The sun has already started to set.
And though I will miss you, I'm glad that we met!
We've had a most enjoyable day.
But now you'd better be on your way."
Mickey tucked his boogie board under one arm,
then picked up the feather to keep as a LUCKY CHARM.

The End.

Come back next season when Sandy Gull's cousin Shellby comes to visit!